Hello, friend! It's time to play!
We're taking care of pets today.

Come with me—I'll show you how.
Turn the page. We'll start right now . . .

Here's a cat who likes to nap.
You can hold her on your lap.
Pat her fur to make her purr—

PURR! PURR! PURR!

This parrot loves to chirp and squawk.
Say "hello" to hear him talk.
What's the word, little bird?

Hello!
Hello!
SQUAWK!

The puppy got all wet and muddy.
Help me wash our little buddy.
Scrub-a-dub—in the tub!

RUFF! RUFF! RRRUFF!

What a helper—you're the best!
Time to take a little rest.

ONE...

Count to three, and stretch with me:

TWO...   THREE...

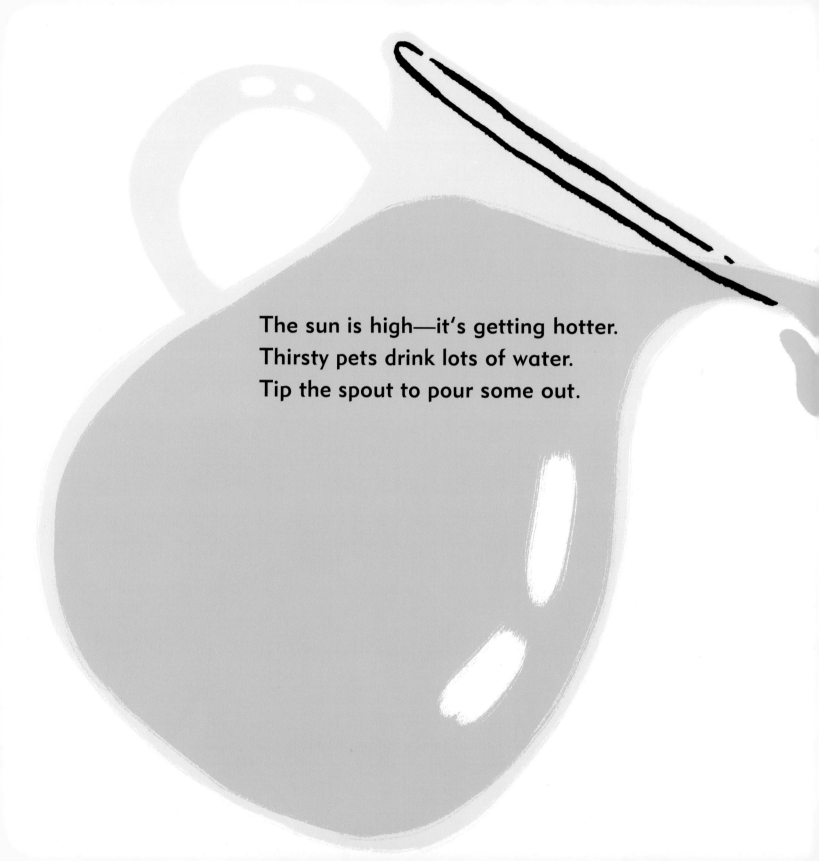

The sun is high—it's getting hotter.
Thirsty pets drink lots of water.
Tip the spout to pour some out.

This hungry lizard needs her lunch.
Give her something good to munch.
Hold a treat for her to eat . . .

Brush the horse's mane and tail,
then take her riding on the trail.
Giddyup! Whoa! Don't let go!

Give a caterpillar space
to hide inside her silky case.

Then wave goodbye,
and watch her . . .

. . . fly!

FLUTTER-
FLUTTER-
FLY!

Thanks for dropping by to play.
We helped a lot of pets today!

Pets need drinks and food to eat,
a wash and brush, a little treat,
a gentle touch, a kind hello,
a friend to care and help them grow,
to keep them safe, or set them free—
someone to love . . .

. . . like you and me!

For Jules and family, and pet lovers everywhere —J. Y.

For Elizabeth and Henry —D. W.

First published in the United States of America in May 2018 by Bloomsbury Children's Books
www.bloomsbury.com

Bloomsbury is a registered trademark of Bloomsbury Publishing Plc

For information about permission to reproduce selections from this book, write to
Permissions, Bloomsbury Children's Books, 1385 Broadway, New York, New York 10018
Bloomsbury books may be purchased for business or promotional use. For information on bulk purchases please contact
Macmillan Corporate and Premium Sales Department at specialmarkets@macmillan.com

Library of Congress Cataloging-in-Publication Data
available at https://lccn.loc.gov/2017033360
ISBN 978-1-68119-507-0 (hardcover) • ISBN 978-1-68119-862-0 (e-book) • ISBN 978-1-68119-863-7 (e-PDF)

Art created digitally with Photoshop, custom brushes, and a lot of bright colors
Typeset in Geometric 415 • Book design by Daniel Wiseman and John Candell
Printed in China by Leo Paper Products, Heshan, Guangdong
1 3 5 7 9 10 8 6 4 2

All papers used by Bloomsbury Publishing, Inc., are natural, recyclable products made from wood grown in well-managed forests.
The manufacturing processes conform to the environmental regulations of the country of origin.

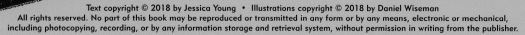